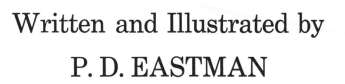

Sam and the Firefly

Written and Illustrated by

P. D. EASTMAN

Beginner Books

A DIVISION OF RANDOM HOUSE, INC.

For Mary,
Tony, and Alan

This title was originally catalogued by the Library of Congress as follows: Eastman, Philip D. Sam and the firefly, written and illustrated by P.D. Eastman. [New York] Beginner Books; distributed by Random House [1958] 62 p. illus. 24 cm. I. Title. PZ10.3.E1095Sam 58-11966 ISBN 0-394-80006-0 (trade); ISBN 0-394-90006-5 (lib. bdg.)

The moon was up
when Sam came out.
"Now is the time for fun," he said.
"who," said Sam, "who!
Who wants to play?"
But no one said a thing.

Then Sam looked about.
The fox was asleep
and the jay was asleep.
The dog was asleep
and the hog was asleep.
The sheep was asleep,
and so was the cow.

Then Sam went down to the lake.
But no one was there.
All he could see was the moon
and the shine of the moon
on the water.
"It takes two to have fun.
WHO," said Sam, "WHO!
Who wants to play?"
But no one said a thing.

Then Sam saw a light!

He saw the light hop.

He saw the light jump.

It went here, it went there.

It went on, it went off.

But no one said a thing.

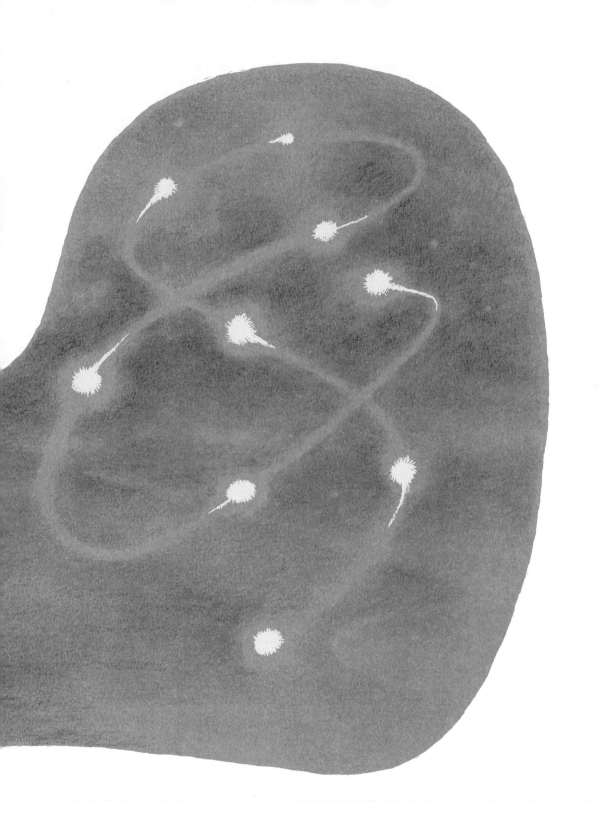

Then the light hit Sam
on the top of his head!
The light said, "BOO!"
"Who made that BOO?" asked Sam.
"Who are you?"

"I am a firefly.

My name is GUS.

And I have a trick I can do
with my light. Look, look!

I can put it on
and KEEP it on,
like this."

Then Sam saw something new!

The firefly made lines
with his light.

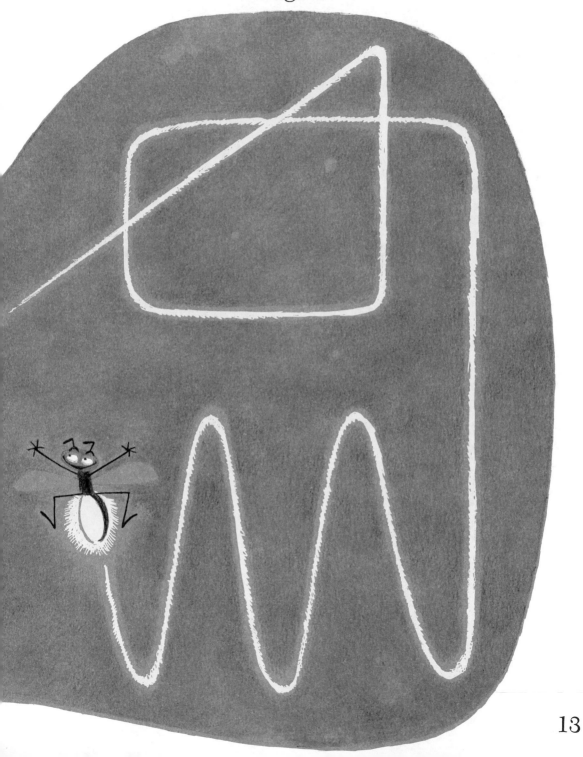

14

"Say!" said Sam.

"WHAT a trick! This is NEW!

Oh, the things we can do

with a trick like THAT!

Let me show you.

Now put on your light

and KEEP it on.

Then you do what I do,"

he said to Gus.

Then Sam went up,
and Gus went after him.
When Sam went down,
down went the firefly too.
Where Sam went,
Gus went.

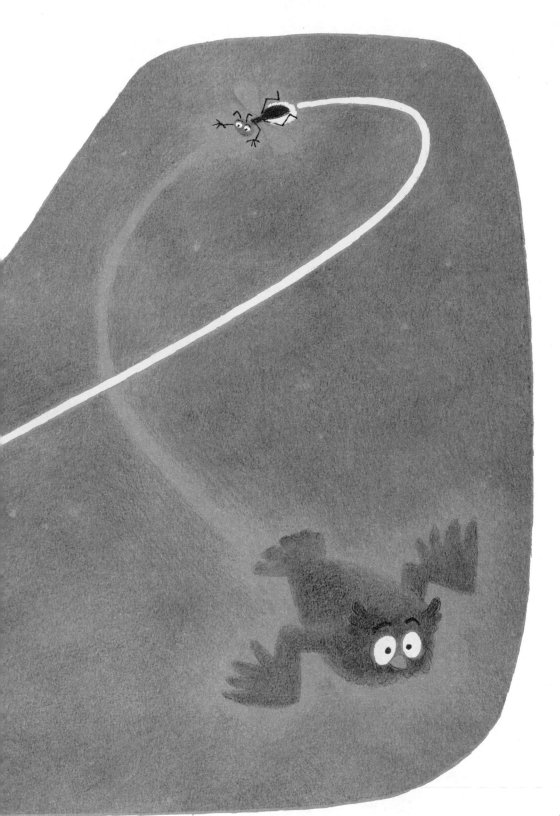

Then Sam stopped,
and Gus stopped too.

"Now just look there," said Sam.

"See what we did!"

GUS AND SAM

"Why! We made WORDS,
BIG words!" said Gus the Firefly.
"Say, I LIKE this game!
I want to do it again.
This word trick is fun.
Come on. Make MORE words."

So away the two went,

Gus after Sam.

They made lots of new words.

They made FISH.

They made WISH.

They made HOUSE

and A MOUSE.

Then

FOX

DOG

CAT

YES

NO

KANGAROO

and THERMOMETER!

FISH WISH
HOUSE A MOUSE
FOX DOG CAT
YES NO
KANGAROO
THERMOMETER

Sam and Gus made a lot
more words.

THEN . . .

21

Sam looked about.

He was all alone!

WHERE was Gus?

Then Sam looked down.

He saw some cars.

And there was the firefly
down by the cars!

"Come back here!" called Sam.

"What are you up to?"

What was Gus up to?

Gus made some words.

Gus made GO FAST and SLOW.

He made GO RIGHT
and GO LEFT.

And DID those cars GO!

They went BASH!

They went SMASH!

Gus did words
that made the cars CRASH.

Oh, what a mess those cars were in!

"Dear me!" said Sam.

"This will not do!

He should not do THIS!

Gus did a bad trick
with those words."

GO FAST GO SLOW
GO RIGHT GO LEFT

25

"Now see here, Gus . . ."

But Gus would NOT see.

He would not hear.

"YOW WOW!

I like to make words,

LOTS of words," he said.

"I LIKE this game!

Let me be, you old GOOSE, you!"

And away he went.

"Stop, Gus! Stop!
Come back!" called Sam.
"That was a BAD trick.
Come back here now.
Bad tricks are not fun!"

"Oh, go on home!" said the firefly.
"You old GOOSE! You old HEN!
What do YOU know about fun?
GOOD-BY!" And away Gus went.

Now Gus did more tricks.

He did word tricks
on some airplanes.

He made them go up.

He made them go down.

He made them go this way.

He made them go that way.

NOW what a mess
the airplanes were in!

"No, Gus! No!" said Sam.

But Gus did not want to stop.

Not yet. This was fun!

Then Sam saw Gus
do another bad trick.

It made the firefly laugh
and laugh.

It was funny
to see them go in free
to the movie show!

"Stop your tricks," called Sam.

"No more words!

Stop, Gus! Stop!

Now STOP!"

33

But Gus the Firefly did NOT stop.

"I have one more trick," he said.

"A LITTLE trick.

Look, Sam! Look!

A ONE WORD trick!"

Then Gus did his little trick,
his ONE WORD trick.

He did a BAD trick

He did it to the Hot Dog Man.

He made the word COLD
near the top of the stand.

The men looked up.

They saw what Gus did.

"We want our Hot Dogs HOT,
not COLD!

Good-by," they said.

Gus did not see the Hot Dog Man,
the man with the net and the jar.

"Look out!" called Sam.

"Look out, Gus!
The Hot Dog Man is MAD!"

"I will GET that firefly,"
said the Hot Dog Man.

"I will take him away from here.
He will not play another
trick on ME!"

Then something hit Gus!
He was in a net!

THEN . . .

GUS THE FIREFLY WAS IN A JAR!

"Let me OUT!"

Gus hit at the walls of the jar!

He hopped about!

He jumped up and down!

But it did no good.

There was no way to get out.

Then Gus in the jar
was in a car!
The car went away fast.
Where would it take him?
Would he do more tricks?
Would he make more words?
Would he have fun again with his light?
Would Gus get out of the jar?

Gus did not know it,
but Sam was there too.
He was near by
in back of the car.
"Oh, what can I do?" said Sam.
"I have to get Gus out of that jar.
But how? How CAN I get him out?"
Sam was sad.

And Gus was sad too.

"I should have stopped
when Sam said NO.

I was bad.

I just had to have fun," said Gus.

"I wish Sam were here
to get me out."

The car went on.

Then it stopped with a BUMP!

49

It stopped on some tracks.

The car would not go!

The Hot Dog Man got out.

Then he looked down the tracks.

What did he see?

He saw a TRAIN!

Sam saw it too!

What would he do?

There was just ONE way

to stop that train!

Sam went to the car.

He took the jar,

the jar with Gus!

THEN . . .

He let the jar fall.

CRASH! And Gus was out!

"You can save the car, Gus!

You can stop the train!

You know what to do!

DO IT!" said Sam.

And the firefly did it!

He made the word STOP.

He did it fast and he did it BIG.

He did it a lot.

He made lots of big STOPS.

"YOW wow, Gus!" called Sam.

"At LAST you did a GOOD trick!"

"Look!

It says STOP!

Look down there!

A car on the track!

STOP THE TRAIN!"

The train DID stop!

And just in time.

"What a trick!" they all said.

"A good, GOOD trick!

HOORAY for the firefly!

He stopped the train!"

But Sam and Gus did not hear.

They had gone away.

Sam looked at Gus
as the sun came up.

"Now the morning light is here,
and no one can see your tricks!

It is time we went home to bed,"
said Sam.

So Sam went back
to his home in the tree,
and Gus went back to the lake.

But night after night,
when the moon comes up,
Gus the Firefly
comes back to play.